Fairy Tales

Fairy Tales

Illustrated by Nikolai Ustinov

Doubleday & Company, Inc.,
Garden City, New York

Contents

Art copyright © Verlag J.F. Schreiber, Esslingen
English translation copyright © 1985 Hodder and Stoughton Ltd.

First Edition in United States of America, 1987
First published in 1984 as *Die schönsten Kindergeschichten*

Library of Congress Cataloging-in-Publication Data

Schönste Kindergeschichten. English.
    Fairy tales.

    Translation of: Die schönsten Kindergeschichten.
    Summary: An illustrated collection of six fairy tales
from six different countries, including the French
"The Magic Thread" and the Spanish "The Three Oranges."
    1. Fairy tales. [1. Fairy tales. 2. Folklore]
I. Ustinov, Nikolai, ill. II. Title.
PZ8.F168598 1987   398.2'1   86-24346
ISBN 0-385-24096-1

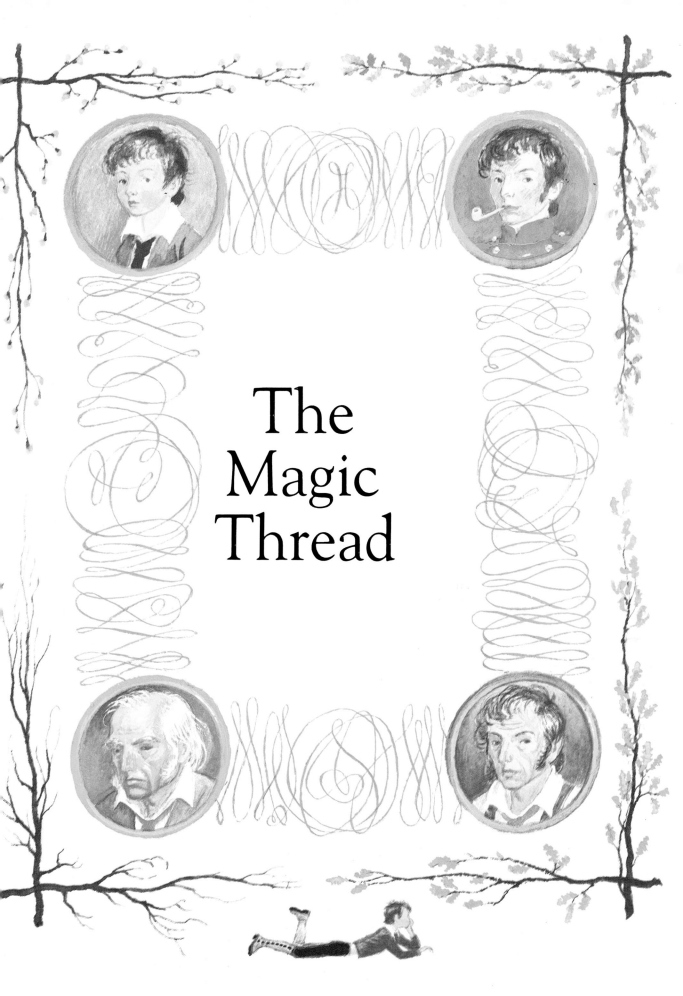

The Magic Thread

Once there was a widow who had a son called Peter. He was a strong, able boy, but he did not enjoy going to school and he was forever daydreaming.

"Peter, what are you dreaming about this time?" his teacher would say to him.

"I'm thinking about what I'll be when I grow up," Peter replied.

"Be patient. There's plenty of time for that. Being grown up isn't all fun, you know," his teacher said.

But Peter found it hard to enjoy whatever he was doing at the moment, and was always hankering after the next thing. In winter he longed for it to be summer again, and in summer he looked forward to the skating, sledging, and warm fires of winter. At school he would long for the day to be over so that he could go home, and on Sunday nights he would sigh, "If only the holidays would come." What he enjoyed most was playing with his friend, Liese. She was as good a companion as any

boy, and no matter how impatient Peter was, she never took offense. "When I grow up, I shall marry Liese," Peter said to himself.

Often he wandered through the forest, dreaming of the future. Sometimes he lay down on the soft forest floor in the warm sun, his hands behind his head, staring up at the sky through the distant treetops. One hot afternoon as he began to grow sleepy, he heard someone calling his name. He opened his eyes and sat up. Standing before him was an old woman. In her hand she held a silver ball, from which dangled a silken golden thread.

"See what I have got here, Peter," she said, offering the ball to him.

'What is it?" he asked curiously, touching the fine golden thread.

"This is your life thread," the old woman replied. "Do not touch it and time will pass normally. But if you wish time to pass more quickly, you have only to pull the thread a little way and

an hour will pass like a second. But I warn you, once the thread has been pulled out, it cannot be pushed back in again. It will disappear like a puff of smoke. The ball is for you. But if you accept my gift you must tell no one, or on that very day you shall die. Now, say, do you want it?"

Peter seized the gift from her joyfully. It was just what he wanted. He examined the silver ball. It was light and solid, made of a single piece. The only flaw in it was the tiny hole from which the bright thread hung. He put the ball in his pocket and ran home. There, making sure that his mother was out, he examined it again. The thread seemed to be creeping very slowly out of the ball, so slowly that it was scarcely noticeable to the naked eye. He longed to give it a quick tug, but dared not do so. Not yet.

The following day at school, Peter sat daydreaming about what he would do with his magic thread. The teacher

scolded him for not concentrating on his work. If only, he thought, it was time to go home. Then he felt the silver ball in his pocket. If he pulled out a tiny bit of thread, the day would be over. Very carefully he took hold of it and tugged. Suddenly the teacher was telling everyone to pack up their books and to leave the classroom in an orderly fashion. Peter was overjoyed. He ran all the way home. How easy life would be now! All his troubles were over. From that day forth he began to pull the thread, just a little, every day.

One day, however, it occurred to him that it was stupid to pull the thread just a little each day. If he gave it a harder tug, school would be over altogether. Then he could start learning a trade and marry Liese. So that night he gave the thread a hard tug, and in the morning he awoke to find himself apprenticed to a carpenter in town. He loved his new life, clambering about on roofs and scaffolding,

lifting and hammering great beams into place that still smelled of the forest. But sometimes, when payday seemed too far off, he gave the thread a little tug and suddenly the week was drawing to a close and it was Friday night and he had money in his pocket.

Liese had also come to town and was living with her aunt, who taught her housekeeping. Peter began to grow impatient for the day when they would be married. It was hard to live so near and yet so far from her. He asked her when they could be married.

"In another year," she said. "Then I will have learned how to be a capable wife."

Peter fingered the silver ball in his pocket.

"Well, the time will pass quickly enough," he said, knowingly.

That night Peter could not sleep. He tossed and turned restlessly. He took the magic ball from under his pillow. For a moment he hesitated; then his impatience got the better of him, and

he tugged at the golden thread. In the morning he awoke to find that the year was over and that Liese had at last agreed to marry him. Now Peter felt truly happy.

But before their wedding could take place, Peter received an official-looking letter. He opened it in trepidation and read that he was expected to report at the army barracks the following week for two years' military service. He showed the letter to Liese in despair.

"Well," she said, "there is nothing for it, we shall just have to wait. But the time will pass quickly, you'll see. There are so many things to do in preparation for our life together."

Peter smiled bravely, knowing that two years would seem a lifetime to him.

Once Peter had settled into life at the barracks, however, he began to feel that it wasn't so bad after all. He quite enjoyed being with all the other young men, and their duties were not very arduous at first. He remembered the

old woman's warning to use the thread wisely and for a while refrained from pulling it. But in time he grew restless again. Army life bored him with its routine duties and harsh discipline. He began pulling the thread to make the week go faster so that it would be Sunday again, or to speed up the time until he was due for leave. And so the two years passed almost as if they had been a dream.

Back home, Peter determined not to pull the thread again until it was absolutely necessary. After all, this was the best time of his life, as everyone told him. He did not want it to be over too quickly. He did, however, give the thread one or two very small tugs, just to speed along the day of his marriage. He longed to tell Liese his secret, but he knew that if he did he would die.

On the day of his wedding, everyone, including Peter, was happy. He could hardly wait to show Liese the house he had built for her. At the wedding feast he glanced over at his mother. He noticed for the first time how gray her hair had grown recently. She seemed to be aging so quickly. Peter felt a pang of guilt that he had pulled the thread so often. Henceforward he would be much more sparing with it and only use it when it was strictly necessary.

A few months later Liese announced that she was going to have a child. Peter was overjoyed and could hardly wait. When the child was born, he felt that he could never want for anything again. But whenever the child was ill or cried through the sleepless night, he gave the thread a little tug, just so that the baby might be well and happy again.

Times were hard. Business was bad

So one day they came and took him away.

His enemies were scattered in a huge explosion.

Liese bore him more children.

and a government had come to power who squeezed the people dry with taxes and would tolerate no opposition. Anyone who became known as a troublemaker was thrown into prison without trial and rumor was enough to condemn a man. Peter had always been known as one who spoke his mind, and very soon he was arrested and cast into jail. Luckily he had his magic ball with him and he tugged very hard at the thread. The prison walls dissolved before him and his enemies were scattered in the huge explosion that burst forth like thunder. It was the war that had been threatening, but it was over as quickly as a summer storm, leaving behind it an exhausted peace. Peter found himself back home with his family. But now he was a middle-aged man.

For a time things went well and Peter lived in relative contentment. One day he looked at his magic ball and saw to his surprise that the thread had turned from gold to silver. He looked in the mirror. His hair was starting to turn gray and his face was lined where before there had not been a wrinkle to be seen. He suddenly felt afraid and determined to use the thread even more carefully than before. Liese bore him more children and he seemed happy as the head of his growing household. His stately manner often made people think of him as some sort of benevolent ruler. He had an air of authority as if he held the fate of others in his hands. He kept his magic ball in a well-hidden place, safe from the curious eyes of his children, knowing that if anyone were to discover it, it would be fatal.

His back and limbs
ached.

As the number of his children grew, so his house became more over-crowded. He would have to extend it, but for that he needed money. He had other worries too. His mother was looking older and more tired every day. It was of no use to pull the magic thread because that would only hasten her approaching death. All too soon she died, and as Peter stood at her graveside, he wondered how it was that life passed so quickly, even without pulling the magic thread.

Liese was often ill.

One night as he lay in bed, kept awake by his worries, he thought how much easier life would be if all his children were grown up and launched upon their careers in life. He gave the thread a mighty tug, and the following day he awoke to find that his children had all left home for jobs in different parts of the country, and that he and his wife were alone. His hair was almost white now and often his back and limbs ached as he climbed the

*The small saplings had
all grown into tall fir
trees.*

ladder or lifted a heavy beam into place. Liese too was getting old and she was often ill. He couldn't bear to see her suffer, so that more and more he resorted to pulling at the magic thread. But as soon as one trouble was solved, another seemed to grow in its place. Perhaps life would be easier if he retired, Peter thought. Then he would no longer have to clamber about on draughty, half-completed buildings and he could look after Liese when she was ill. The trouble was that he didn't have enough money to live on. He picked up his magic ball and looked at it. To his dismay he saw that the thread was no longer silver but gray and lusterless. He decided to go for a walk in the forest to think things over.

It was a long time since he had been in that part of the forest. The small saplings had all grown into tall fir trees, and it was hard to find the path he had

once known. Eventually he came to a bench in a clearing. He sat down to rest and fell into a light doze. He was woken by someone calling his name, "Peter! Peter!"

He looked up and saw the old woman he had met so many years ago when she had given him the magic silver ball with its golden thread. She looked just as she had on that day, not a day older. She smiled at him.

"So, Peter, have you had a good life?" she asked.

"I'm not sure," Peter said. "Your magic ball is a wonderful thing. I have never had to suffer or wait for anything in my life. And yet it has all passed so quickly. I feel that I have had no time to take in what has happened to me, neither the good things nor the bad. Now there is so little time left. I dare not pull the thread again for it will only bring me to my death. I do not think

your gift has brought me luck."

"How ungrateful you are!" the old woman said. "In what way would you have wished things to be different?"

"Perhaps if you had given me a different ball, one where I could have pushed the thread back in as well as pulling it out. Then I could have re-lived the things that went badly."
The old woman laughed.

"You ask a great deal! Do you think that God allows us to live our lives twice over? But I can grant you one final wish, you foolish, demanding man."

"What is that?" Peter asked.

"Choose," the old woman said.
Peter thought hard. At length he said,

"I should like to live my life again as if for the first time, but without your magic ball. Then I will experience the bad things as well as the good without cutting them short, and at least my life will not pass as swiftly and meaning-lessly as a daydream."

"So be it," said the old woman. "Give me back my ball."

She stretched out her hand and Peter placed the silver ball in it. Then he sat back and closed his eyes with exhaustion.

When he awoke he was in his own bed. His youthful mother was bending over him, shaking him gently.

"Wake up, Peter. You will be late for school. You were sleeping like the dead!"

He looked up at her in surprise and relief.

"I've had a terrible dream, mother. I dreamed that I was old and sick and that my life had passed like the blink-ing of an eye with nothing to show for it. Not even any memories."

His mother laughed and shook her head.

"That will never happen," she said. "Memories are the one thing we all have, even when we are old. Now hurry and get dressed. Liese is waiting for you and you will be late for school."

As Peter walked to school with Liese, he noticed what a bright summer morning it was, the kind of morning when it felt good to be alive. Soon he would see his friends and classmates, even the prospect of lessons didn't seem so bad. In fact he could hardly wait.

King Turnip Counter

Many years ago in the great mountains of Bohemia there lived a Dwarf King, who became known as King Turnip Counter. He disliked this name intensely because it reminded him of how he had once been tricked and made a fool of by a young princess. He bore the grudge for the rest of his days. This is how it happened.

Each summer the King of Bohemia brought his court to the great mountains to escape the stifling heat of the plains. It was cool in his lovely summer palace. There were gardens to play in, lakes to swim and fish in, and woods and green hills for rides and picnics. The mountain villagers looked forward to the arrival of the king and his court because they brought life and excitement. Fairs and fêtes were held in the market places, and many people came to trade and to catch glimpses of the

courtiers in their finery. And so the villages prospered and the king was popular with his people and was held to be a just and generous overlord. It was a time of peace and contentment in the land.

The king had a daughter called Angelica. She was just eighteen and as lovely as a newly opened rosebud. With her came her friend, Brunhilde, who was the same age and almost as beautiful as the princess. The two girls played and danced all day long and far into the long summer night. And the following morning, soon after the sun rose, they were up again ready to ride out into the forest, and swim, and dance some more. Sometimes they galloped for miles, to the farthest hills. There they dismounted from their horses to let them rest and drink from a mountain pool, whilst they themselves picked armfuls of wildflowers. Once or twice, when the day was hottest, they swam in the deep dark water, deeper and darker than the blue sky overhead.

One day the two girls were resting on the grass beside their grazing ponies, when suddenly the Dwarf King came out of the trees and saw them there. Quickly, not wanting to be recognized, he changed into a wandering student. The girls looked up at his approach. He doffed his cap and bowed low in greeting. Angelica smiled at him and at once his heart was touched as it had never been before. From that moment he began to plot how he could have the beautiful girl for himself. He returned to his kingdom and puzzled about how to capture her. He poured over books of magic and ancient wisdom, and at last he decided upon a way to take her.

A few weeks later it was Angelica's birthday. A great ball was planned for the evening and lords and ladies from far and wide had been invited.

Angelica grew more and more excited as the day approached. She wondered whether among the many handsome young noblemen who would be at the ball, she would find the man she was going to fall in love with and marry. On the morning of her birthday, people began to arrive early with their gifts. There were gifts of silk and silver, emeralds and pearls, a white cockatoo who called her name, "Angelica!", and from Brunhilde a little white kitten with china blue eyes and a tail held straight above his silky back, like the plume in a soldier's cap. From her mother Angelica received seven ball gowns: one pink, one blue, one yellow, one of palest green, one deep violet like the midnight sky, one silver, and the last and most lovely, a pale shimmering white, the color of the milky moon. Then her father called her to come and look at his gift. Outside in the courtyard, a white Arab horse tossed its head. His mane and tail flowed almost to the ground, and his bridle and saddle were of red leather, tooled in gold.

"I must ride him at once," cried Angelica, clapping her hands in delight. "Come, Brunhilde."

Together, accompanied by several of their friends, they rode out into the forest and beyond, to the far hills, until they reached the mountain pool where Angelica and Brunhilde had met the Dwarf King. The girls dismounted, eager for a swim because the day was already hot. Then they saw to their amazement that the steep, stony rim of the pool was banked with cushions of soft moss, and that instead of gloomy

fir trees, the water was edged with silver birches and blossoming shrubs. Flowers carpeted the ground and birds sang joyfully in the trees. At the far side of the pool they saw a dark hole like a yawning, toothless mouth. Waves lapped its entrance and from its mysterious depths colored light flickered, like the glitter of precious stones.

The girls stared at it in fascination.

Angelica walked to the edge of the pool, and began to wade into the water. Instead of sharp stones beneath her feet, her toes felt the smooth coolness of marble. She waded deeper until she was up to her waist. Seeing her, her friends called out to go no farther into that strange pool. But she answered that she was not afraid, and waded on until the water reached her shoulders. Then suddenly she disappeared, as quickly as if the ground had opened up and swallowed her. Brunhilde cried out in horror. Running to the water, she dived in and began to search for her. The others clustered around the water's edge, calling her name again and again. But there was no sign of her. Unable to bear the cold of the water any longer, Brunhilde returned sadly to the shore. At length, not knowing what else to do, the party turned wretchedly for home, to tell the king and seek his help in finding Angelica.

The king fell into despair at the news. He sent out divers to search for his daughter, but they returned saying that they had been unable to find the pool. At this the king's last grain of hope faded, for he believed that his daughter was now dead and gone forever. But the queen could not believe that she would never see her child again and sent a proclamation throughout the land, promising a rich reward and their daughter's hand in marriage to any young man who could find the lovely Angelica. In her heart she suspected that her daughter's disappearance had something to do with the Dwarf King, but she said nothing for fear of being laughed at.

Meanwhile Angelica fretted in the Dwarf King's kingdom. The chilly marble floor of the mountain pool had indeed opened up, and she found herself standing on a path, silvery bright as if lit by moonlight. In front of her stood a tall young man, dressed as a nobleman.

He bowed deeply.

"I am the king of the dwarfs," he said. "My kingdom stretches for many hundreds of miles beneath these mountains. It has castles, waterfalls, lakes, and gardens of great beauty, and treasure immeasurable. You shall be its Queen and reign here beside me. I shall give you whatever you want, you have only to name it."

Angelica stared at him. He was not ugly, nor was his look unkind. But she had no wish to stay there forever, away from her home, family, and friends. She remembered hearing that the Dwarf King could change his form whenever he wished. She was entirely in his power and did not want to anger him. So she said, "I must have time to get to know you before I give you my answer. And I need the permission of the king, my father."

The Dwarf King was content that she had not refused him at once, and readily consented to her request for time.

"Meanwhile I shall show you some of the marvels of my kingdom," he said. "Once you have seen them, you

will no longer want to return to the world above."

He snapped his fingers, and at once an army of tiny servants appeared. With their nimble fingers, they quickly fashioned a rich garment in which they dressed Angelica, and a pair of jewelled slippers for her feet. Wearing these she was able to fly through the halls and passages of the palace like a bird. When she grew tired of this, the Dwarf King called for one of his noblemen, who took her onto his back and flew with her out of the palace, through the gardens to the waterfalls and underground lakes, where great tree roots from the upper world twisted about the rocks. In the underground woods there were many animals of the kind that Angelica recognized, bears, deer, rabbits and squirrels. But none of them seemed to be afraid of her. The bears did their stately dance for her, and the stag let her ride upon his back.

But despite all these wonderful things, Angelica grew sadder and sadder and more and more homesick. She missed her parents and her dear friend, Brunhilde, and wondered if she would ever see them again. Sometimes she thought that Brunhilde would lead her father and his knights to the mountain pool and that they would be able to find her and rescue her. At others she

felt that they would never find her and, believing her to be drowned, would give up the search so that she would have to remain there forever.

Seeing her sadness, the Dwarf King asked her what was the matter.

"I am lonely," she said. "If only I had my dear friend, Brunhilde, and some of the courtiers to talk to, I should not feel so bad."

"That is easy to arrange," said the Dwarf King.

The following day he brought her a basketful of turnips. He handed her a small wand, saying, "With this wand you can turn the turnips into whoever you wish. Say the name of the friends

you miss most and they will stand before you. Only you cannot bring forth your parents for they are a royal king and queen."

Angelica was overjoyed, and as soon as he was gone, she touched the first turnip with the wand and uttered the name "Brunhilde!" At once her friend stood before her and they threw their arms around one another, laughing and crying for joy. Then Angelica touched each turnip in turn, uttering the names of different friends and playmates and several of the young noblemen of the court, even the court jester. Now that she was no longer alone, Angelica was almost able to forget that

they still remained prisoners in the Dwarf King's kingdom.

But very soon her friends began to fade and grow weak. Afraid for them and seeking to do them good, Angelica took them out to the underground woods and lakes. She watched them as they wearily dismounted from their horses. They seemed to be withering before her very eyes.

"What is the matter with you?" she cried to Brunhilde in despair. But Brunhilde's voice was too weak and hoarse to reply.

Angelica rode back to the Dwarf King as swiftly as she could.

"What is the matter with my friends?" she said angrily. "They shrivel and die. If I lose them, I will never agree to be your wife."

"What do you expect of turnips?" the Dwarf King said. "But have patience, my princess. I will bring you fresh turnips and you can create your friends anew. Only now it is winter above ground and the earth is covered with snow. You must wait a little while for the turnips to ripen."

Day by day Angelica watched her friends grow weaker and more wizened no matter how she tried to cheer them. At last she could bear to see them no longer. She touched each one with her magic wand, starting with Brunhilde,

and at once they became dried up, withered turnips.

Meanwhile the Dwarf King had set his dwarfs to labor building great fires under the frozen turnip fields in an effort to speed up the turnips' ripening. Every day he went to see how they were getting on, so that Angelica was left alone. She often thought of escape, and one day she called for a stag and rode away to the farthest limits of the Dwarf King's kingdom. There the land emerged from underground and ended in a wide strip of rough water, and on the other side of it, she could see the forests and mountains of her father's kingdom. She was filled with a desperate homesickness, but suddenly she

was distracted by the sight of a young man standing on the far shore. He appeared to be staring over at her, his hand shading his eyes.

"Who are you?" she called, waving to him and hoping that he would be able to hear her.

"I am Prince Reinhart," he called back. "I am searching for the Princess Angelica. If you have any knowledge of her, please tell me at once for I would give my life to find her."

"I am she!" Angelica replied in great excitement. "But I must not stay now. The Dwarf King will be looking for me, and he moves with the speed of lightning. Wait here until I return with two swift horses."

And with that she turned and rode back into the underground kingdom, leaving the prince in great turmoil on the farther bank.

As she approached the Dwarf King's palace, he hurried to meet her, carrying two turnips.

"Where have you been? I've been looking for you. Look, the turnips are ripe. Tomorrow my dwarfs will harvest them and you may create a whole court full of people for yourself."

"That is good news," said Angelica. "But will you grant me one favor."

"Name it," said the Dwarf King.

"Will you tell me exactly how many

turnips there are, so that I may know whether I can create my father's court exactly, down to the last kitchen maid?"

The Dwarf King was not accustomed to counting, having more than enough of whatever he needed, but he agreed, seeing that it would please Angelica.

"You must not make a mistake," she said. "If you did, I should know you to be more stupid than I thought, and I could not marry a stupid husband."

The Dwarf King hurried away to prepare for the harvesting of the turnips. But Angelica took the two that he had brought her and touched them with her magic wand, saying, "I command you to turn into two swift horses."

And at once they did so.

She mounted one, and leading the other by the reins, she galloped off toward the farther limits of the Dwarf King's kingdom.

She rode all night, while the Dwarf King counted the turnips he had harvested. Each time he counted them, the sum came out slightly different. But at last he felt sure that he had got the number right, and hurried back to the palace to tell Angelica. When he got there, he found that she was nowhere to be seen. He hunted high and low for her, until he realized how she had tricked him. Then he was seized with rage, a violent anger that blew away all his love for her. All he wanted was revenge, and that he was determined to get.

He snatched up his magic cloak and soared into the air. He flew with the speed of light to all corners of his kingdom, but there was no sign of her. Then at last, he caught sight of something moving below him. It was Angelica astride a horse, struggling in the rough water against the powerful current. Behind her swam another horse, and on the far shore stood a young man, cheering them on. She was almost at the shore, but the Dwarf King, snarling with rage, plucked a lightning bolt out of the sky and hurled it at Angelica. It almost hit her, but at that moment she reached the land and the young man pulled her to safety. The lightning bolt entered the water and shivered into a thousand pieces.

He knew that he had been outwitted and, with a cry of disappointed rage, he wheeled around and re-entered the darkness of his kingdom.

The prince caught Angelica as she slipped, exhausted, to the ground and held her in his arms. But there was no time to delay, and as soon as she had caught her breath, they set off again on horseback for her father's palace. It was a long and tiring ride through the mountains, and they dared not stop or sleep for fear that the Dwarf King might find some way to follow and attack them. To distract themselves from their weariness, they told each other tales of their adventures, and by the time they were nearing home, Angelica was as much in love with Prince Reinhart as he already was with her.

At last they were in sight of the palace. It was summer again in the land of Bohemia, and the king and queen stood sadly in their drawing room, its long windows open on to the lawn, where the evening shadows were stretched. The king seemed to have grown old in his despair, but the queen often thought of their child and could not believe that she was really dead. Suddenly they heard dogs barking and the sound of voices and people running in the courtyard. The queen called Brunhilde to go and see what all the commotion was about. In a moment Brunhilde returned, her eyes alight with joy.

"Come quickly," she said to the king and queen. "You will never believe it, but Angelica has returned! And with her Prince Reinhart."

The king and queen hurried to the courtyard, scarcely able to believe their ears. There they saw that it was indeed their lost child who had returned, and they embraced her with tears of joy, and none of them could get their fill of looking at the other, so glad they were to be together again.

A few weeks later, Angelica and Prince Reinhart were married. So, at the same time, were Brunhilde and Prince

The king and queen stood in the glow of the evening light.

Reinhart's younger brother. The two young couples lived in neighboring castles so that they were often able to go riding and fishing together, just as Angelica and Brunhilde had done for so many years, though they never again bathed in the mountain pools. As for the Dwarf King, he continued to grow angry whenever he thought of how the human princess had tricked him. For many years he did not venture out of his dwarfs' kingdom, and when at last he did so, he found to his shame and annoyance that he was known as "King Turnip Counter" by the mortals above ground.

The Dwarf King continued to grow
angry whenever he thought of how the human princess
had tricked him.

Cap O'Reeds

Once there was a powerful king who was generous and kind so long as his will was obeyed. He had three beautiful daughters and when the time came for them to marry, the princes they had chosen came to the king to ask him for his daughters' hands in marriage.

"Who will look after me when I'm old and feeble if you leave me?" the king said to his daughters. "I have no one else in the world but you. You must wait until after I am dead."

The two eldest daughters were angry with their father and the youngest felt sad and sick at heart. But none of them dared question their father's word.

The time came when the king felt too old to rule any longer.

"I am a tired old man," he said. "It is time that I should step down from my throne. I shall divide my kingdom into three parts and you will rule in my place. I, together with a hundred of my knights, shall stay a month with each of you in turn. And to whoever loves me best I shall give the richest and loveliest third of my kingdom." The king turned to his eldest daughter.

"Tell me now, daughter, how much do you love me?" She hesitated for a moment, then began to speak.

"I love you, father, better than the whole world. In comparison to this, the world and all its riches are nothing to me. Come first to me and I will look after you in the royal way that suits your greatness." The king smiled and turned to his second daughter.

"And what about you, my dear?" he asked. "How much do you love me?" She answered without delay.

"I love you more than life itself. I shall marry only so that I may have a home to offer you. Therefore, father, come at once to me and I will care for you until the end of your days."

The king smiled again, satisfied by his daughter's answer. Then he turned to his youngest and favorite child.

"Now, my daughter, tell me how much you love me."

But his youngest daughter frowned and looked down and answered,

"I have nothing to say, father."

"Nothing!" the king roared.

"Very well, I love you as it befits a daughter to love her father."

"Take care, my child. Think again about what you say."

"To be without you, would be like eating food without salt," she said.

"Get out of my sight, you ungrateful

child! You, to whom I would have given everything! Well, you can beg for your living. You will get nothing from me. I shall divide my kingdom between your sisters, and you shall leave this palace so that henceforth I need never set eyes on you again."

With that the king got up from his throne and left the Hall.

The court, trembling, whispered to one another. But the two eldest princesses turned to their sister and said, "Well, sister. I wonder whether your prince will be so keen to marry you now that you are penniless?"

And indeed that night the young prince packed up his things and quietly made his way from the palace back to his own kingdom, leaving only a note for the young princess explaining that though he deeply regretted it, he could not marry a girl who was penniless.

The following day the youngest princess also left the palace, weeping

and broken-hearted. She was allowed to take nothing with her except for three dresses: one ordinary dress, one special dress, and her wedding dress. Many of the courtiers wept to see her go, but her sisters did not shed a tear, and their father snapped at the servants and refused to watch her leave.

When she had gone a little way from the palace, the young princess came to a wide river, banked with reeds. She picked some and wove them into a coat to cover her dress and protect it from the weather. Then she made a cap of reeds to keep the rain from her head. The people who saw her called her Cap O'Reeds. And so she wandered on for many months, sleeping wherever she could find shelter, eating whatever

food she was offered, until at length she came to another kingdom and a large, bustling town.

The kingdom was ruled over by a young and handsome prince, whose father had recently died, so that now the young man was looking for a queen to rule beside him. But his search for a bride was half-hearted because he could not forget the princess whom he had truly loved but had abandoned. The memory of his faithlessness tormented him and he longed to see her again.

When she arrived at the young king's palace, Cap O'Reeds went around to the kitchen door and asked to be taken to the cook.

"Have you some work for me?" Cap O'Reeds asked the cook. The cook

looked her up and down in her strange coat and reed cap.

"We have plenty of servants here, but you look so hungry and wretched that I will see what I can do for you."

And she set her to wash dishes, scrub floors, empty slops, and other menial tasks, for which she received food and a bed in the attic with the other kitchen maids. It was a hard life and often at night Cap O'Reeds was almost too tired to climb the stairs to bed.

Meanwhile the old king, her father, had gone to visit his eldest daughter, together with his hundred knights. Very soon the riotous behavior of his knights exasperated her beyond endurance so that she went to her father and said, "Father, your knights have turned my house from a gracious palace into a tavern. You have no need of so many. Fifty would be quite sufficient. The rest must be told to leave my kingdom."

"What, daughter, do you order me

to get rid of my knights when I willingly gave you half my kingdom? You are hard and ungrateful! I will not stay here a moment longer, but will go at once to your sister." And with that he left and traveled to the palace of his second daughter.

"What are you doing here?" she asked him. "Your month with my sister isn't up yet."

"She insisted that I get rid of half my knights, so that I said that I would no longer stay in her house but would go where I knew that I and my men would be welcome. And here we are."

His daughter frowned.

"But, father, we are not prepared for

you yet. However since you are here you had better stay, but I cannot have a single one of your knights."

"Unfeeling woman!" the old man cried. "You are even harder than your sister. At least she left me fifty of my knights. And to think I gave you everything!" So he turned back and wearily retraced his steps to his eldest daughter's palace.

But when he and his men arrived, they found the gates locked and barred against them. They banged on them and shouted. The princess and her husband appeared on the battlements.

"We have twice as many soldiers as you. Go away while you can or we

shall be forced to come out and fight you," they called down.

Hearing this, the knights knew that they were defeated and, bidding a sad farewell to their king, fled away to their own parts of the country.

Now the king was quite alone. He had nothing except the horse he rode upon and this, though he sorely regretted it, he had to sell for food. Carrying his provisions with him, he walked away into the forest, and after many days of wandering, he came to a deserted hut in the middle of a clearing. He rested there for a few days and when no one returned to take possession of the hut, he decided to make it his home.

Though he did not know it, the old king had wandered into the country where his youngest daughter now lived. The clearing in which his hut stood was not far from the young king's palace. Sometimes the old king heard the sound of huntsmen riding through the forest and dogs barking. Sometimes too the kitchen maids came into the forest to gather berries and mushrooms. One day the old king was sitting in front of his hut in the afternoon sunshine, when a young girl came into the clearing. She stood stock still, staring at him in astonishment, for she recognized her old father. She came toward him, struggling to hide her strong feelings.

"Are you alone, old man?" she asked.

"Yes," he answered, smiling at her because he was glad to see a friendly face. But he had grown so short-sighted and confused that he did not recognize his daughter, disguised as she was by her coat and cap of reeds.

"Shall I stay and talk to you for a little while? Perhaps I could cook for you or wash your clothes?" she asked. The old king accepted her company and her help with gratitude, and she began to visit him regularly, whenever she could escape from her kitchen duties. The old man began to look

forward to her coming with an eagerness that grew with each visit.

A few weeks later, the young king decided to hold a great feast. All the servants were invited to watch the celebration, but Cap O'Reeds was ordered to watch over the food in the kitchen until it was needed.

"You can't be seen by the king's guests in such strange clothes," the cook said.

When the servants had all gone to the Great Hall, Cap O'Reeds ran upstairs to the attic, took off her coat and cap of reeds and put on her ordinary dress which, being the dress of a princess, transformed her utterly. She came into the Great Hall. The young king saw her standing in the doorway, the most beautiful girl he had ever seen, yet with something vaguely familiar about her.

"Do I know you?" he asked.

She smiled without answering him, and soon he forgot his question as they began to dance together.

For the whole evening the young king danced with the strange girl, whom nobody seemed to recognize. Then, before the last dance, she slipped away while the king's attention was distracted for a moment, and when he turned back to her she was gone. No one had seen her leave.

At length, in despair, the king decided to hold another feast in the hope that she might appear once more. Again the servants were given leave to attend the celebrations, all except Cap O'Reeds. And again, as soon as she was alone, she ran up to the attic, took off her coat and cap of reeds, and put on her special dress. She looked even lovelier than before.

As she entered the Great Hall there was a gasp of excitement from the guests and the king hurried to greet her. He led her by the hand to the dance floor and danced with her all evening or sat beside her, offering her the choicest morsels from the banquet. During the last waltz he bent his head to hers and whispered, "You are the most beautiful woman I have ever seen. Will you marry me?" She looked at him and smiled but said nothing.

Later, as the king said goodbye to his guests, who were starting to leave, Cap O'Reeds moved quietly away to the door.

The king, not dreaming that she could be part of his own household, ran into the streets, searching up and down and calling for her. But she had disappeared. In the early hours of the morning he returned home, exhausted and utterly disconsolate.

In desperation the cook inquired of

the kitchen maids if any of them knew of a dish that might tempt the unhappy king. Cap O'Reeds said that there was one from her country that might possibly do the trick. When it was ready and the footman had carried it in to the king, to his astonishment the king tasted it, then ate it all down. At the bottom of his bowl lay a ring. He stared at it in wonder, knowing it as the betrothal ring that he had given to his lost princess.

"Where did this come from?" he cried. "Fetch me the cook at once!"

The cook hurried back to the kitchen and told Cap O'Reeds to tidy herself quickly because the king wanted to see her. She ran up to the attic room and put on her wedding dress. Then she put back her coat and cap of reeds so that they covered her dress and her gleaming hair, and went downstairs to the king.

"Tell me how this ring came to be lying in the bottom of my bowl?" He held it out for her to see.

"I put it there," she said.

"Where did you get it from?"

"A prince gave it to me."

The king stared at her troubled and thoughtful.

"What is your name?" he asked.

"People call me Cap O'Reeds."

"Take off your curious garments," the king said, pointing to her coat and cap of reeds.

She took off her cap, and her bright hair tumbled to her shoulders. Then she took off her coat of reeds and stood before him in the brilliance of her wedding dress.

The king went to her and took her by the hand.

"So, it is you! Can you ever forgive me for what I have done?"

"Yes," she said, "for you too have suffered."

All the bells in the city rang out for the wedding of the young king and his princess. After the ceremony there was to be a great feast to which all the king's subjects were invited, even the old man who lived in the forest. Cap O'Reeds had gone to him in her coat and cap of reeds and asked him to come, though he had no idea who the bride was going to be. Then the princess went to the cook and said, "Please do not put any salt in the dishes for the wedding feast."

At the wedding feast the young queen sat with her husband on one side of her and the old man from the forest on the other. She watched her father as he took his first mouthful of food. He grimaced with disappointment at its tastelessness, then tears began to flow down his withered cheeks.

"What is the matter?" the young queen asked him.

"I was remembering my beloved youngest daughter," he said. "Once I

foolishly asked her how much she loved me and when she replied, 'As much as food needs salt,' I drove her from my house in rage. I was blindly arrogant, and now I would give anything to find her and beg her forgiveness."

The young queen took the old king in her arms and said, "Father, it is I, the daughter whom you seek." So they all rejoiced, giving thanks that they had found one another again. Soon after, the young king and queen raised a great army to go into the old king's country to quell the fighting that had broken out between the two eldest daughters. In the end the whole country came under the rule of the young king and queen. They ruled it justly and wisely so that the people prospered after the hardship of the eldest sisters' era. The old king lived in their palace with the young king and queen, where he had a hundred knights to attend him. And so they all lived happily ever after.

The Seven Doves

Once there was a poor widow who lived on the bank of a river with her seven sons and her baby daughter, Anna. Her sons were growing up and they wanted to go out into the world to seek their fortunes.

"Do not worry, Mother," said the eldest son, "we will soon be back to

take care of you and our little sister." And off they went. Years passed, but they did not return. The mother grieved for them. She was sure they were dead.

But this was not so. The brothers traveled all over the country, stopping first in one place and then in another, earning their living and seeing the world. Finally the time came when they had had enough of traveling and they turned around and headed for home. They decided to return by the shortest route, but this meant crossing a great, dark forest where a terrible giant lived. Everyone feared him for he liked to catch people and eat them. The brothers tried to avoid him but, although he was nearly blind, he heard their footsteps on the forest path and suddenly appeared before them.

"Fee, fie, fo, fum," the giant roared, "tasty morsels for my supper." "Please, sir," said the eldest brother, "If you spare our lives, we will stay and work for you."

The giant thought for a moment and then he agreed. "You can live here and take it in turns to lead me about," he said. "My cat will keep an eye on you, and woe betide you if you try to escape."

When Anna was eighteen, she decided to find out what had happened to her brothers, so she said goodbye to her mother and set off down the road her brothers had taken. Many people remembered the seven travelers and told Anna which way to go, and so it was that one day she came across the little house in the forest where her brothers lived. When her brothers saw her, they were delighted.

"Come in quickly," they said. "Don't let the giant see you. If you stay here with us you will be safe, but when we are away, always remain in the house. Take care too not to anger the giant's cat. He could do you harm."

Anna settled down and lived happily with her brothers. She looked after the house and was careful to avoid the giant. One day, when she was alone in the kitchen, she absentmindedly put some sausage in her mouth, quite forgetting to give a piece to the cat. The cat was furious. It hissed and spat and pulled the coals from the fire. Forgetting her brothers' warning,

Anna went out into the garden to fetch fresh wood. Unluckily for her, the giant was walking through the forest. He sniffed the air and looked toward her. Anna ran back into the house, slammed the door and threw the wood on to the fire. But the giant came up the garden path, broke down the door, and blundered into the kitchen. He was just about to catch Anna, when her brothers came back.

"Quick, giant," said her youngest brother craftily, "this way! The stranger has escaped through the front door."

The giant turned and ran out of the house but because he could not see, he tripped and fell into a deep ditch full of water and was drowned. As quick as lightning, the brothers filled the ditch with earth. They went to catch the cat, but the cat gave a shrill cry and disappeared through the trees. Anna was saved! Then the brothers gave their sister another stern warning. She must never pick the herbs that grew about the giant's grave, for if anyone

should eat them, they would turn into a bird. Anna promised that she would remember.

Now they could all live happily. In spring, they planned to go home to their mother. But a dreadful thing happened. One day, while the brothers were out in the forest, chopping wood, an old man came and knocked on the door. He told Anna that he had hurt his head so Anna hurried to fetch herbs to put on his wound and rosemary to make him some tea and she did not notice that they grew close to the giant's grave. She bandaged the old

man's head and he hurried on his way. A few minutes later, the brothers came home, tired and cold, and when they saw the tea on the table, they drank it. Within minutes, there were sounds of fluttering and mournful cries. The seven brothers had turned into seven doves.

"Anna, Anna," one of them wept, "how could you forget? Now we will be doves for the rest of our lives," and they flew through the window and perched on a tree in the garden.

Anna was in despair. She did not know what to do so she went to a wise

woman and asked her advice. The wise woman said, "You must go to the house of Time and ask her to help you. She will not want to listen to you but if you remove the weights from her pendulum clock, she will lose her power and will have to grant your every wish. You must make sure that she swears on her wings that she will not harm you. It is the only way you can be protected from her revenge."

"How do I find her?" asked Anna.

"You must ask your way," said the wise woman.

Anna took her coat and a bag of grain and set off, accompanied by the seven doves.

She walked for many hours and eventually reached the seashore. There on the sand lay an enormous whale who asked Anna, "What are you looking for, little landlubber?"

"I am looking for the house of Time," replied Anna. "Go along the beach," said the whale, "until the path stops by the cliff. There you will find someone to help you on your way. But could you do me a favor? When you find Time, ask her how I can avoid being thrown onto the rocks."

"Certainly," said Anna and on she went. She was quite exhausted by the time she reached the cliff. A little mouse scurried by and asked, "Where are you going?"

"I am looking for the house of Time," replied Anna. The mouse said, "Go over the blue mountain to the great plain. Cross the plain and there you will find someone who will help you on your way. But could you do me a favor? When you find Time, ask her what I can do to protect myself from the cat."

Anna promised that she would and lay down on the mountain path to rest. The doves clustered close to her and, in spite of the cold, she managed to sleep. Early next morning she set off to

climb the mountain and cross the plain.

At the very end of the plain, she came to an enormous oak tree and it said, "Rest in my shade, little human." "Thank you," said Anna, "but I cannot stop. I have to find the house of Time. Do you know where she lives?"

"Over there, in the trees," said the oak. "But could you do me a favor? I used to be respected by men, but now pigs have been allowed to sniff at my bark and trample my roots. When you find Time, ask her how I can regain my lost honor." Anna promised that she would and hurried on with the doves fluttering about her.

The house was very old and very strange, and the front door was shut. An old man lay huddled in the shade nearby, and to Anna's surprise she saw that it was the old man whose head she had bandaged.

"What are you doing here?" she asked. "Oh," said the old man, "I came to ask Time for a few more years, but she won't listen to me." "What will you do now?" asked Anna. "I plan to ask her once more. She is sleeping, but she will soon be awake, she has so many things to attend to." "What does she look like?" asked Anna. "She has gray hair, a pointed chin, wings on her back, and a wrinkled face," replied the old man.

"How can I get inside?" asked Anna. "There is a little door at the back," said the old man, "but I dare not use it."

Anna called the doves to her and crept quietly around to the back door. It was open. There on the wall was a pendulum clock, just as the wise woman had said. She carefully stopped the pendulum and hid the weights away. With the doves behind her, she crossed the hall and tiptoed into the parlor. There on a couch, half-covered by her powerful wings, Time seemed to lie sleeping. Anna looked at her in astonishment. The short rest must have made her young again, her face was soft and round, and her hair had regained its color. Time opened her eyes and stared at Anna.

Then she cried, "Why are you in my house, wretched girl?" Anna's heart was beating fast but she hid her fear and said, "Noble Time, I ask you to grant my wishes." "Wishes! What do I care for wishes," said Time. "Go, if you hold your life dear." "You cannot harm me," said Anna. "I have stopped your clock." Time looked at her angrily. "Speak," she said, so Anna listed all the wishes she had gathered on her journey.

"Very well," said Time. "Turn these seven doves back into my brothers," said Anna.

"Come here," said Time, and she touched each of the doves lightly with her wings. And there, to Anna's joy, stood her brothers again.

"Now put back the weights on my clock," commanded Time. Anna did so, but when she turned to thank her, there was no one there. Anna and her brothers ran outside. Time had clearly kept her promise for the old man no longer stooped but was joyful and vigorous again.

They walked through the trees and came to the oak. "Look!" said the oak.

"Time came to me. She told me that robbers had buried a crock of gold beneath my roots and brought shame upon me. Please, would you dig it up?"

The brothers did so and the oak gave them the gold as a present. Later they came to the cliffs and there they found the mouse. "Look!" cried the mouse. "Time came to me. She told me to hang a bell around the cat's neck when she is asleep. I shall never be caught unaware again!"

Anna gave the little mouse her bag of grain. Suddenly seven fierce robbers appeared. They tied Anna and her brothers to a tree and ran off with the crock of gold. The mouse, however, managed to gnaw through the rope to set them free and told them where the robbers had hidden the gold. Quickly they found it and set off along the seashore. They came to the whale.

"Look!" said the whale. "Time came to me. She told me to make friends with the dolphin. He knows the coast. Things will be better for me now!"

As he spoke, the robbers came running up again, furious to find their gold missing. "Help us," cried Anna in alarm.

"Quick," said the whale, "climb on my back and I'll take you home." And

that is what happened! The whale took them across the sea to the mouth of the river, and there on the bank was their house. Their mother and every one of her neighbors ran out to greet them. How pleased she was to see them safe and home again, and what a great celebration they had that night!

The Three
Oranges

There was once a poor widow who had three sons. The sons wished to be married, yet none of the village girls appealed to them. In a cottage just beyond the village, lived an old woman. The villagers were a little afraid of her because, though she was known to be wise, they suspected that she liked to eat not merely bread and wine, like everyone else.

One day the three brothers went to visit her to ask if she could find each of them a wife.

"What sort of a wife do you want?" the old woman asked.

"A beautiful one," the eldest brother said.

"A rich one," the second brother said.

"What did you ask us?" said the youngest brother vaguely.

The others laughed at him for being so stupid, but the old woman repeated her question. He thought for a moment, then said, "I want a wife whom I shall love with all my heart, as she will

love me."

The brothers laughed again, but the old woman said, "Each of you will get the wife he desires. But you must all stand by one another and do exactly as I say. If you travel east for three days, you will come to a castle. Outside the castle is an orange orchard, and among the many trees you will find one tree which has only three ripe fruits, the biggest and most beautiful fruits in the orchard. You must pick them quickly or you will be captured by the lord of the castle and never return home again. But take care that in doing so, you do not damage the tree. When you have picked the oranges, bring them to me and each of you shall have his wife."

The following morning they set off in search of the castle. They traveled all day and at night slept in a deserted barn. During the night, the eldest brother was wakened by the moon shining through the rafters onto his face. His brothers were asleep and he said to himself, "If I went now, I could get there first and take the best orange for myself. If I wait for the others, who knows how long the journey will take and how many arguments we may get into on the way. I shall go to the castle, pick my orange, and return to the old woman on my own. The other two can follow after."

And with that he got up, crept out of the barn and set off quickly for the castle.

He traveled so fast that he arrived there the following evening. Before the castle was a garden full of orange trees. The trees were so laden with fruit that the garden glowed golden in the moonlight. The gate stood open and the young man slipped inside. There was no sign of life from the castle.

For a long time he searched for the orange tree with three fruits. Then at last he saw it—a mighty tree in the corner of the orchard, covered half in blossom, half in unripe fruits. But on one of its branches hung three perfect oranges, shining as if they had been polished. He stretched up to pick one, but he was unable to reach the branch.

"If only my brothers were here, then we could climb on one another's shoulders," he said to himself. He started to climb the tree, but placing one heavily booted foot upon a branch, it snapped and broke off just as he was reaching out to grab an orange. He tried to climb down again but found that he was stuck fast, unable to move.

At that moment lights came on there was the sound of shouting from the castle. The castle gate burst open

and soldiers rushed out, making for the orchard. They surrounded the tree where the eldest brother was, and an old man appeared, for whom they made way. He prodded the eldest brother with his stick and the young man suddenly found that he could move again. He climbed down from the tree. At once the soldiers seized him, marched him off, and threw him into a dungeon underneath the castle.

That same morning, the two other brothers had woken up to find the eldest gone. They set off quickly to follow him. But they did not travel so fast as he did and had to spend another night, bedded down in an old

shepherd's cart. It was cramped and uncomfortable, and during the night the second brother awoke. He looked at his brother, peacefully asleep, and said to himself, "Our eldest brother will already have reached the castle by now. He will take the best fruit for himself if I don't hurry up and catch him. Our younger brother is a fool and will spoil everything. It would be better if I left him to follow us on his own."

So he climbed quietly out of the cart and set off again, traveling for the rest of the night until he reached the castle on the following morning.

The orchard gate stood open, and the

second brother walked in. Ahead of him he could make out a faint path trampled in the grass.

He followed it, and it led him straight to the mighty tree, where three perfect oranges hung, glowing in the sunshine. He looked up at them, thinking to himself, "If only my brothers were here, then we could climb on one another's shoulders and reach the fruit."

Then he noticed the broken branch and realized that it would not be safe to climb the tree. He looked around for something to beat the oranges down with. There was a stick lying in the grass. He picked it up and began beating at the tree, but at that moment

there was a great commotion from the castle, and soldiers rushed out and seized him. They threw him into a dungeon with his brother.

The youngest brother awoke, surprised to find himself alone. He shook his head anxiously, saying to himself, "I must hurry up and get to the castle. My brothers may be in danger and in need of my help."

He traveled all day and at evening arrived at the castle. The orchard was bathed in moonlight. He saw a path and followed it until he came to a mighty tree. There, among the blossoms and the unripe fruit, hung three, glossy oranges.

He stared at them and thought, "But how can I get them without damaging the tree?"

He backed away, took a run at the tree and leaped high into the air. He grabbed at an orange and managed to grasp it. But as he fell back to earth, he realized that he had pulled down the branch with the fruit, and small cries, as though of pain, came from the tree. At that moment the castle gate opened and an old man walked solemnly out. He was dressed as a nobleman, and his expression was serious and sad.

"So you have got the three oranges," the old man said. "They will protect you, but because you have torn off the branch as well, many sorrows will befall you."

And with this, he turned and went back into the castle.

The youngest brother followed him. When he came to the closed castle gate, he touched it with his orange branch and at once it swung open. Cautiously he entered the castle. He found himself in a magnificent hall, elegantly furnished with portraits of noble men and women along the walls. Each door he came to, he touched with his orange branch and at once it sprang open. Eventually he reached the cellar and there came upon a row of dungeons, in one of which he found his two brothers. They were overjoyed to see him and ashamed of having left him alone. There was nothing in the dungeon except three loaves of bread and three flasks of wine, which had been placed upon a shelf. The brothers took a loaf and a wine flask each, the youngest brother touched the door of the dungeon with the orange branch so that it sprang open, and together they crept up through the castle without meeting anyone. Once beyond the castle gates, they hurried home, carrying the branch with the three oranges with them.

After traveling for several hours, they sat down to rest. The two eldest

When the youngest brother awoke that morning . . .

. . . he was surprised to find himself alone.

brothers felt hungry and thirsty and ate up all their bread and drank down their wine. The youngest brother, however, felt refreshed by merely smelling the wonderful fragrance of the oranges. Despite the heat, the leaves on the branch had not withered, nor had the oranges begun to dry up or to lose any of their glossy sheen. The brothers lay back in the shade to sleep until the heat of the day was over. But when, a little later, the eldest brother awoke, he was consumed by such a thirst and a restless desire to be gone so that he could get back to the old woman, that he got up and looked around for some water. There was neither a stream nor a village in sight, so he reached out and plucked an orange from the branch. He took out his knife and split it in two. Out sprang a beautiful girl. He stared in wonder and admiration.

"Have you any bread I can eat?" she asked him.

"I have already eaten it," he said regretfully.

"Have you any wine I can drink?"

"I have already drunk it," he replied, hanging his head.

"In that case I will go back into my orange and return to the tree," the girl said, and she disappeared at once as if she had never been. The eldest brother stood there, shaken and amazed, and

seized by soldiers and thrown back into the dungeon. This time he was alone and terribly frightened. But the soldiers had provided him with a few comforts: food, wine, and an oil lamp to cheer the darkness. He took a drink from the wine flask. It tasted good and warmed his stomach, so that he began to feel a little more hopeful.

One evening the silence of his cell was interrupted by the sound of keys jangling in the lock. The door opened and he saw a young woman enter his cell. She stood, illumined by a glow, not of candles but from the many jewels that adorned her. On her glossy black head she wore a crown of diamonds; diamonds sparkled in her ears and at her wrists from the jewelled cuffs that encircled them. On the fingers of each hand, she wore rings heavy with precious stones. The pearl necklace at her throat was simple in comparison with the rest of her finery. She sat down on the stool opposite the eldest brother and smiled at him.

"Time passes slowly for you," she said.

He wanted to reply, "No longer," but he was unable to say a word. He could only stare at her. He could not decide whether she was plain or beautiful. All he could see were the jewels, which outshone any beauty the girl

when he had gathered himself, he was filled with longing to see the girl again. He could not bear the thought that he had found her, only to lose her at once. So he turned back and hurried off in the direction of the orchard.

It took him a long time to reach the castle because, in his haste, he took many wrong turnings on the way. Eventually, however, he got there, but no sooner did he do so, than he was might have possessed. They sat on in silence. At length he said to her, "You have so many beautiful jewels. Would you give some of them to the poor so that they might build a hospice for their dying and their sick?"

"Certainly I will," she said. "In a little while you may have need of it yourself."

And with that, she got up and left.

The guard who locked the door after her, put his head back into the cell and said, "What a fool you are! If you had chosen her, you would be a free man now."

But the eldest brother replied, "No, it would only have been another prison."

And he was left alone in the darkness.

The night after the eldest brother had left, the second brother awoke with a raging thirst. Unable to find anything to drink, he took the branch from his younger brother, cut off an orange, and slit it open. At once a girl stood before him, dressed from top to toe in fine clothes, sparkling with jewels. Even her shoes had gleaming diamond buckles.

"Have you any bread I can eat?" she asked him.

"I have already eaten it," he replied.

"Have you any wine I can drink?"

"I have already drunk it," he said sorrowfully.

"In that case I will go back into my orange and return to my tree." And at once she vanished into thin air.

Like his brother, as soon as the second brother had recovered himself, he hurried back in the direction of the orchard.

After taking many wrong turnings in his haste, he eventually reached the castle. But as soon as he did so, the

*Have you any bread
I can eat?*

*Have you any wine
I can drink?*

soldiers seized him and threw him into a dungeon. After some hours, he heard the jangling of keys in the lock, and the cell door swung open. The guard ushered in a young girl. She was simply dressed but of wondrous beauty. Long silken hair framed her exquisite face, falling to her slender waist, and her figure was lithe as a young tree. He stared at her in wonder and admiration. Yet how could he choose such a delicate creature, who would have to be protected and cared for in a way that he was too poor to do, and who would be surrounded by scores of wealthy admirers. The girl saw his troubled face.

"I have mistaken this door for another. Forgive me," she said.

Then she got up and left.

The guard who ushered her out put his head back into the cell and said scornfully, "What a fool you are! If you had chosen her, you would be a free man now."

And he was left alone in the darkness.

Meanwhile the youngest brother awoke in the morning to find himself alone and only one orange left on the branch. He said to himself, "Now both of them have gone off to see the old woman. I will have to hurry if I am to catch up with them."

He had not gone far when he was

*"You have found yourself a
pretty little bride"*

She took hold of the head of the pin and carefully drew it out

overcome by thirst. He took out his knife and cut into the orange. Out sprang a young girl. She stood before him, plainly dressed, with a sweet, lovely face, and such a look of tenderness that he thought he would die of love for her.

"Have you any bread I can eat?" she asked.

He nodded, broke off a piece of bread, and gave it to her. She ate, then turned to him again.

"Have you any wine I can drink?"

He nodded again and poured some wine into his cup from his wine flask. He handed it to her and she drank it down. When she had finished, she poured some more wine into the cup and handed it back to him.

"Now we shall be happy together," she said.

When they reached the old woman's cottage on the outskirts of the village, the youngest brother explained to her what had happened.

"You disobeyed my instructions and broke off the branch," the old woman said. "You will suffer for this."

Then she turned to the girl.

"But at least you have found yourself a pretty little bride." And she went up to the girl and kissed her. As she did so, she drew out a pin from her shawl and drove it into the back of the girl's head.

The girl shrieked in terror and vanished. In her place fluttered a white dove, which hovered about the young man anxiously.

The young man searched high and low, but there was no sign of her. The old woman had disappeared too and he was alone, except for the white dove which continued to flutter around him. Despairingly he turned his steps in the direction of his mother's house.

She grieved for her two eldest sons and for the bride that her youngest son had lost. Yet she took comfort from the fact that at least she had one son safely home. The two of them lived quietly together with the white dove, which refused to leave them.

One morning the mother noticed that the dove kept scratching its head with its feet. She ran her fingers over its downy head and suddenly felt something sharp.

"Someone has driven a pin into the head of this little creature. Whoever could have done such a thing?" She took hold of the head of the pin and carefully drew it out. At once the dove turned back into a girl. The son looked at her with joyous amazement.

"It is my bride!" he cried out, and took her in his arms.

A little later, the girl looked around for the orange branch.

"I threw it away, thinking it was rubbish and no longer needed," he said.

"We must go back to the castle at once," the young girl said. "There we will find everything that we have lost."

In less than two days they had reached the orange orchard in front of

the castle. The youngest son saw to his surprise that the branch he had torn from the orange tree had grown back again, and two fine fruits hung upon it. A stick lay in the grass beside the tree, but he did not pick it up. Instead he knelt down and said to the girl, "Climb up on my shoulders and then you can reach the oranges."

She did so and picked them and

climbed down again. No sooner had she done so than they turned into the two beautiful girls that the eldest brothers had already seen.

At that moment the castle gate flew open and the old man and his soldiers strode out. With them they brought the two eldest brothers. Seeing them, the youngest brother's bride took a

hand of each of her sisters and led them towards the brothers. She placed the hands of each girl in those of her intended bridegroom. Then the old man went over to the orange tree and touched the branch with his stick. At once it fell from the tree and turned into a beautiful woman.

"This is my wife, the mother of these three girls," he said. "In an angry rage I banished her to the orange tree, together with my daughters. Now at last they are free, and I am released from my torment."

And so the three brothers were married. Each of them was happy because he had just what he wanted. But the youngest brother was the happiest of all.

The Witch's Swans

Once upon a time there was a rich farmer who lived on the edge of the village with his wife, daughter, and little son. One day the mother said, "Daughter dear, we are off to market. We will bring you back a loaf of fine, white bread and a pretty dress. But make sure you look after your little brother while we are away. Don't let him out of your sight."

No sooner had her parents set off, than the girl completely forgot her mother's instructions. She took her brother down to the meadow, sat him on the grass and went off to play with her friends. Suddenly there was a swishing sound in the sky and, looking up, she saw a flock of wild swans hovering above her. They swooped down low, one of the swans seized her brother, and then the whole flock flew off toward the forest.

The girl cried out in despair and started to run across the meadow after them. On her way, she saw a bread oven.

"Bread oven," she cried, "tell me where the wild swans live."

"I will tell you if you eat some of my bread," the oven replied.

"I don't want to eat your black bread," the girl said scornfully. "My father gives me my fill of fine, white bread." The bread oven was silent so she ran on.

Soon she came to a wide stream. "Dear stream," said the girl, "tell me where the wild swans live."

"I'll tell you if you drink some of my water," replied the stream. "I don't want to drink river water," said the girl rudely. "My father gives me my fill of

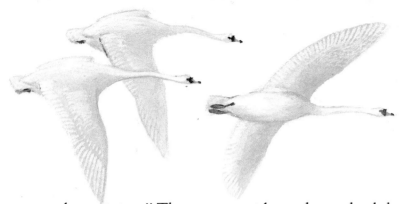

sweet raspberry juice." The stream said nothing and so the girl ran on.

Soon she came to a crab apple tree. "Crab apple tree," said the girl, "tell me where the wild swans live."

"I will tell you if you eat some of my apples," replied the crab apple tree. "I don't want to eat your sour little apples," said the girl. "My father gives me the sweetest apples from his garden." The crab apple tree said nothing and so the girl ran on.

She would have gone on running for

hours had she not met a hedgehog who told her the wild swans lived in a hut half-hidden in the trees. The hut was built on stilts and, through the open window, the girl could see a witch sitting, drinking tea. Outside on the grass sat the girl's little brother playing with some apples.

The girl dashed over, grabbed the child and ran back through the wood. The witch rushed out of the house with her broomstick and started to chase them, but the girl ran so fast that soon

the witch was left behind. So the witch called up her swans and they took to the air and flew after the girl.

She came to the crab apple tree and cried, "Dear crab apple tree, help me, hide us!"

"Will you eat my apples this time?" said the tree.

The girl gladly obeyed, and the tree spread out its leafy branches and hid them from the swans. But when the girl hurried on again, the swans caught sight of her and flew after her. She came to the wide stream. "Dear, sweet stream," she said, "help me, hide us!"

"Will you drink my water this time?" said the stream.

The girl drank gladly for her throat

was dry from so much running. The stream led her to a deep hollow which had been formed by its current, and the swans flew past. But when the girl ran on, they saw her once again. They swooped down, beating their powerful wings, and would have caught her in their beaks had she not caught sight of the bread oven. "Dear, sweet bread oven, help me, hide us!" cried the girl.

"Will you eat my bread this time?" said the bread oven.

Quickly the girl put a piece in her mouth and, holding her brother tight, jumped inside. The swans circled overhead, seeking and calling, but they could not find the girl and her brother. And finally the swans gave up and flew back into the forest.

The girl ran home as fast as her legs could carry her, and she was only just in time for at that very moment her parents arrived back from market.